D1261709

The World of Fashion

Fashion
DESIGN SCHOOL

2

Learning the
Skills to Succeed

by Jen Jones

Consultant: Cherie Bodenstab
Assistant Department Chairperson
Fashion Design Department
The Fashion Institute of Design & Merchandising (FIDM)
Los Angeles, California

Capstone
press®

Mankato, Minnesota

Snap Books are published by Capstone Press,

151 Good Counsel Drive, P.O. Box 669, Mankato, Minnesota 56002.

www.capstonepress.com

For information regarding permission, write to Capstone Press,
151 Good Counsel Drive, P.O. Box 669, Dept. R, Mankato, Minnesota 56002.

Printed in the United States of America

Library of Congress Cataloging-in-Publication Data

Jones, Jen, 1976–

Fashion design school: learning the skills to succeed / by Jen Jones.

p. cm.—(Snap books. The world of fashion)

Summary: "Describes fashion design schools and classes and the skills
needed to succeed"—Provided by publisher.

Includes bibliographical references and index.

ISBN-13: 978-0-7368-6832-7 (hardcover)

ISBN-10: 0-7368-6832-1 (hardcover)

ISBN-13: 978-0-7368-7886-9 (softcover pbk.)

ISBN-10: 0-7368-7886-6 (softcover pbk.)

1. Fashion design—Vocational guidance—Juvenile literature.

2. Fashion—Vocational guidance—Juvenile literature. I. Title. II. Series.

TT507.J665 2007

746.9'20711—dc22   2006021847

Editor: Amber Bannerman
Designer: Juliette Peters
Photo Researcher: Charlene Deyle

Table of Contents

Introduction
Dare to Dream 4

Chapter One
Designing Your Future:
Your Path to the Professional World 6

Chapter Two
Bag of Tricks:
The Skills You Need to Succeed 14

Chapter Three
The Real World:
Life After Design School 22

Glossary 30

Fast Facts 30

Read More 31

Internet Sites 31

About the Author 32

Index 32

Dare to Dream

If you've got a flair for fashion, a promising design career could be yours. However, competition is tough in the clothing business. In 2004, there were only about 17,000 working designers in the United States. The people who want fashion jobs outnumber the jobs available. The good news is that design school gives you an advantage.

Design schools train young artists for jobs in fashion. In this book, you'll discover the secrets of getting accepted. You'll also get the real deal on what classes and jobs are like. A bright future awaits!

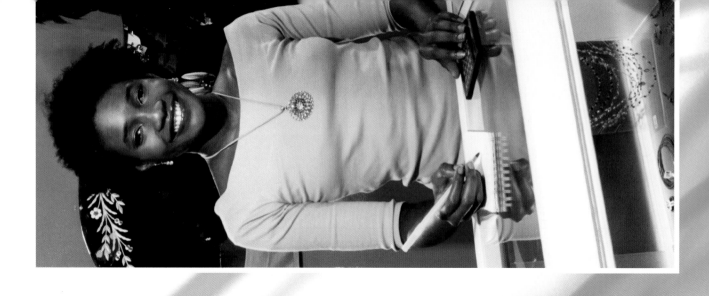

Chapter One

Designing Your Future: Your Path to the Professional World

You may be thinking, "I haven't even started high school. I'm not ready to think about college!" The great news is that your future is wide open. There are many ways to explore your fashion curiosity. Before walking through the college doors, you could:

- Work at a retail store.

- Talk to local fashion designers.

- Keep a sketchbook of ideas.

You could even tour fashion design colleges. By the time you're old enough to be a student, you'll be on familiar territory!

School's In

The Fashion Industries High School (FIHS) in New York isn't your everyday high school. Students study fashion design, merchandising, and art illustration. Window displays line the building's front, making it look like a department store. The FIHS also has a small student-run clothing store and a yearly fashion show.

Decisions, Decisions

Studying fashion design is a great path for those who are artistic and love clothes. Choosing the right design college is like searching for the perfect outfit. You want it to be a great fit! Just like you choose clothes based on style, size, and cost, many things can affect your school decision.

Location

In 2004, two-thirds of designers worked in New York or California. Studying design in these places puts you at the heart of the business.

Faculty

Your teachers will play a big part in your education. Take time to research their backgrounds. Have they worked for major clothing companies or spent years designing their own clothing lines? You just may follow in their footsteps!

Cost

If cost is a concern, choose a public college. A two-year program would also be a smart money move.

Credit Check

Last but not least, reputation should be considered. Luckily, the National Association of Schools of Art and Design (NASAD) has done some homework for you. About 250 U.S. schools are accredited by the NASAD. These schools meet educational standards set by the group.

The Fashion Institute of Design & Merchandising, Orange County Campus, CA

The Golden Ticket

To high school seniors, no two words sound better than "You're accepted!" But getting into a design school can be tough. Unlike many colleges, grades and test scores don't make or break your chances. Instead, creativity and skill play an important part.

One way to stand out from the crowd is to create a killer portfolio. A portfolio is a collection of sketches. It shows off your style ideas and drawing skills. For instance, at The Fashion Institute of Design & Merchandising (FIDM) in Los Angeles, a portfolio must include ten clothing illustrations. The artwork must range from evening gowns to sportswear.

Tuition prices often rise by up to 10 percent each year. Financial aid can be a huge help. Many students apply for grants, scholarships, and loans from the government. Community groups such as 4-H clubs and church organizations also may offer aid. Tap into your local network!

Those who are unable to raise enough money sometimes spend a year working. This approach lets future fashion students get real-life experience while saving for school.

Get with the Program

An old saying goes, "Life is not a destination. It's a journey." This saying could be handy to keep in mind. There are many paths you can take to reach your goal of being a designer.

For the fashion-minded, a four-year fashion school could be your calling. The classes are built around knowledge needed to get ahead in the fashion world. Schools such as FIDM offer classes like fashion sketching, computer-aided fashion design, and history of costume.

Life is not a destination. It's a journey.

Some students are itching to enter the "real world." They might want a shorter course of study at a trade school. For up to two years, students take "hands-on" classes. They prepare for very specific careers like alteration specialist, fashion illustrator, or visual display artist.

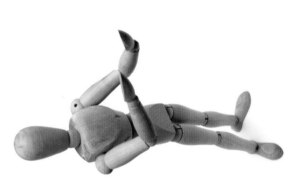

Other students may want to pair their study of fashion with other interests. In that case, many public and private colleges offer fashion design majors. While taking fashion classes, students can major or minor in other areas like art or business.

Depending on the program, you will receive a degree or certification upon completing it. Hats off to those who do!

Chapter Two

Bag of Tricks: The Skills You Need to Succeed

Successful fashion designers have it all. They've got an eye for style, a brain for business, and a skilled hand for art. Learning about art is the smartest thing a designer can do. The better your designs look on the page, the better they'll look in real life!

In fashion drawing classes, students draw clothed models. They may use pencils, charcoal, colored markers, or ink to make their sketches. Drawing actual people helps students understand human proportions. Students also learn how to show clothing details and movement.

Art history classes connect fashion students with the past. At the same time, they inspire students for the future. Learning about designers who've paved the way can help you carve your own path to fame.

Color theory classes teach students how different colors work together. This knowledge comes in handy when designing multi-colored or patterned clothes. It makes the difference between a complement and a clash.

Tune Up Your Tech Skills

Paper and pencil are powerful design tools. Yet technology is the wave of the future. To keep up with new trends, students must learn computer-aided design, or CAD. CAD lets designers easily make changes to their work. They no longer have to go "back to the drawing board."

At the Parsons School of Design, students move through four levels of the fashion digital studio course. In the classes, software such as Adobe Photoshop and Illustrator is used. Students create fabric and clothing designs on the computer. Some students also take graphic design and Web design courses.

The Fabric of Your Career

In design school, there is rarely a dull moment. Many classes involve much more than just taking notes. Clothing construction courses show students how to actually make the outfits they've designed. Learning by doing is the name of the game!

Sewing and knitting classes are full of activity. Students practice these skills by hand and machine. In draping classes, students practice fitting fabric to dress forms.

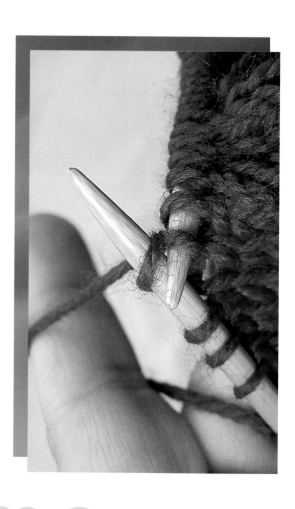

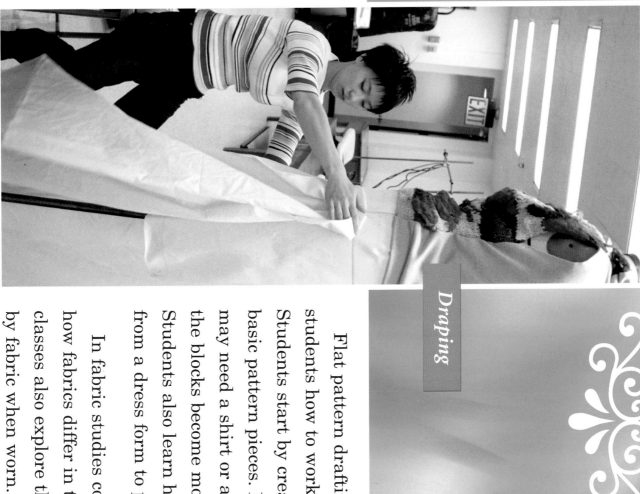

Flat pattern drafting classes teach students how to work with measurements. Students start by creating simple "blocks," or basic pattern pieces. For example, students may need a shirt or a pants block. Later, the blocks become more detailed patterns. Students also learn how to transfer drapes from a dress form to paper.

In fabric studies courses, students find out how fabrics differ in texture and quality. The classes also explore the silhouettes created by fabric when worn.

Jill of All Trades

Becoming a designer is like a juggling act. Designers always have many "balls in the air." They need to bring their creations to life. They must also know how to market them successfully. For that reason, a design student must branch out with a well-rounded set of classes.

Future designers study "the three M's:" merchandising, manufacturing, and marketing. These topics show students the inner workings of the industry. Students learn how clothes are mass-made, advertised, and sold. They also study the costs of producing clothing. This helps them plan costs for their own future clothing lines.

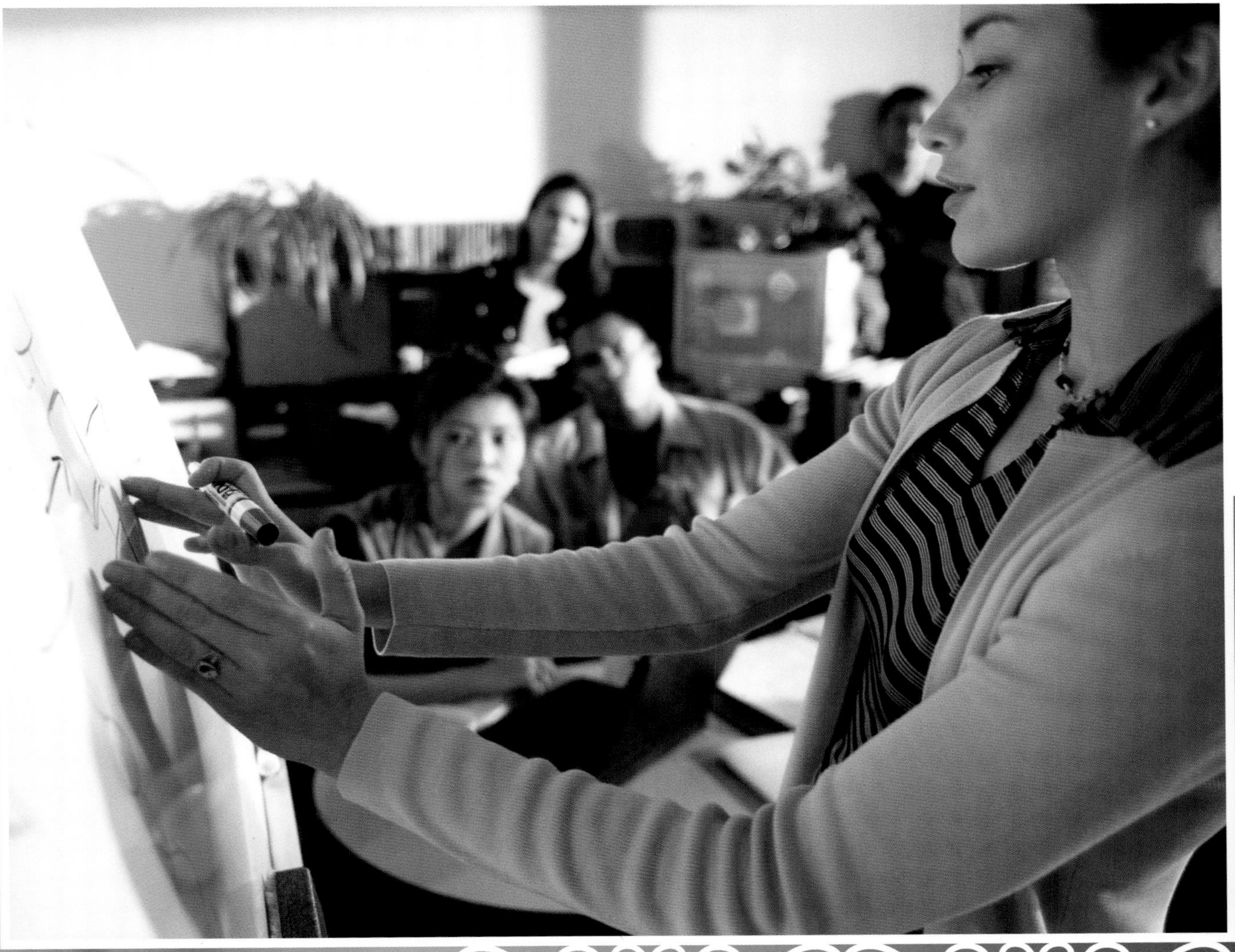

The Real World: Life After Design School

Want to take your career for a test drive? Do an internship! Internships take students out of the classroom and into the workplace. Though internships pay little to nothing, they give you an opportunity to get your feet wet. They can even lead to full-time work after graduation.

Many students go overseas for internship programs. They journey to "fashion capitals" like Milan, Italy, or Paris, France. But don't worry if you can't afford to travel the globe. You can find internships in your own town. From tiny boutiques to famous fashion design firms, the choice is yours!

Me and My Shadow

Fashion design apprenticeships allow young designers to work with a well-known designer. Unlike an internship, an apprenticeship can last several years.

Famous designer Tommy Hilfiger with his team

Once complete, a young designer has experience and a great collection of contacts. And better yet, not every apprenticeship ends with the words "You're fired," à la Donald Trump's reality show, *The Apprentice*. In the real world, they often end with "You're hired!"

Humble Beginnings

Many now-famous designers began as apprentices. Gianni Versace kept his apprenticeship "all in the family." He got his start at his mother's dressmaking business in Italy. At the young age of 15, high-end designer Stella McCartney helped Christian Lacroix with his first couture collection.

Join the Club

Looking for scholarships, design colleges, or networking opportunities? Trade associations hold the key. These groups are for working professionals and future designers. Becoming a member lets you meet and get advice from the best. You'll also get your hands on job leads, insider information, and special events. Plus, membership looks great on a résumé.

**2006 CFDA *award winner*
*Doo-Ri Chung***

The Council of Fashion Designers of America (CFDA) is one association that's worth knowing about. The CFDA offers a masters program. In it, selected graduating college students complete a one-year internship. College students can also go to CFDA discussion panels that cover what it's like to be a young designer in the business and other related topics.

CFDA Awards

Who doesn't like to win an award—especially when it's a cherished award from the CFDA? Each year, the CFDA presents awards to people from all walks of the design industry. The Swarovski's Perry Ellis Award is awarded to up-and-coming designers. Doo-Ri Chung won this important award for her womenswear in 2006. Well known for her draped jersey dresses, Chung produces fashionable, low-maintenance styles.

The Finish Line

After a rewarding design school experience, what comes next? With diplomas in hand, thousands of graduates find themselves in this position every year. Most young designers start their careers in apprenticeships or entry-level jobs.

With all the competition, new designers might feel discouraged. If you ever feel this way, remember that top designers were once in your shoes. Calvin Klein and Norma Kamali graduated from the Fashion Institute of Technology. Donna Karan and Anna Sui both got their degrees from Parsons School of Design. With hard work and a positive attitude, your career can take off too!

Fast Facts

Former FIDM scholarship student Monique Lhullier now designs luxury wedding gowns for celebrities.

Tennis star Serena Williams studied fashion design at the Art Institute of Florida.

Many stars use their fame to pursue their dream of being fashion designers. They know their fans might be interested in buying their designs. Some celebrities who've created clothing lines include Jessica Simpson, Beyoncé Knowles, and Nicky Hilton.

Glossary

boutique (boo-TEEK)—a small unique store

couture (koo-TUR)—fashionable custom-made women's clothing

merchandising (MER-chen-diz-ing)—the promotion, buying, and selling of goods

portfolio (port-FO-lee-oh)—a book or collection of artwork

proportion (pruh-POR-shuhn)—the relation of one part to another

résumé (RE-zuh-may)—a written summary of a person's work history, education, awards, and other important experiences

silhouette (sil-oo-ET)—an outline of something that shows its shape

Read More

Hufford, Deborah. *Fashion Crafts: Create Your Own Style.* Crafts. Mankato, Minn.: Capstone Press, 2006.

Jones, Jen. *Fashion Careers: Finding the Right Fit.* Mankato, Minn.: Capstone Press, 2007.

Peterson, Tiffany. *Fashion Designs.* Draw It! Chicago: Heinemann, 2003.

Rakel-Ferguson, Kat. *Artistic Drawing.* Creative Kids. Cincinnati: North Light Books, 2002.

Internet Sites

FactHound offers a safe, fun way to find Internet sites related to this book. All of the sites on FactHound have been researched by our staff.

Here's how:

1. Visit *www.facthound.com*
2. Choose your grade level.
3. Type in this book ID **0736868321** for age-appropriate sites. You may also browse subjects by clicking on letters, or by clicking on pictures and words.
4. Click on the **Fetch It** button.

FactHound will fetch the best sites for you!

Index

apparel construction, 18
apprenticeships, 24–25
art history, 15

color theory, 15
computer-aided design (CAD), 16
Council of Fashion Designers of America (CFDA), 27

draping, 18
drawing, 14

fabric studies, 19
Fashion Industries High School (FIHS), 7
Fashion Institute of Design & Merchandising (FIDM), 11, 12, 30
flat pattern drafting, 19

internships, 22, 27

knitting, 18

marketing, 20

Parsons School of Design, 16, 28
portfolios, 11

school considerations
  cost, 9, 11
  faculty, 8
  location, 8
  reputation, 9
  sewing, 18

tours, 6
trade associations, 26–27
types (of schools), 12–13

About the Author

Jen Jones has always been fascinated by fashion—and the evidence can be found in her piles of magazines and overflowing closet! She is a Los Angeles-based writer who has published stories in magazines such as *American Cheerleader*, *Dance Spirit*, *Ohio Today*, and *Pilates Style*. She has also written for E! Online and PBS Kids. Jones has been a Web site producer for *The Jenny Jones Show*, *The Sharon Osbourne Show*, and *The Larry Elder Show*. She's also written books for young girls on cheerleading, knitting, figure skating, and gymnastics.